Pillow

Pillow

Exploring the Heart of Eros

A *Yellow Silk* Book by
LILY POND

CELESTIAL ARTS
BERKELEY, CALIFORNIA

Celestial Arts
P.O. Box 7123
Berkeley, California 94707

Distributed in Canada by Publishers Group West, in the United Kingdom and Europe by Airlift Books, in New Zealand by Tandem Press, in Australia by Simon & Schuster Australia, in Singapore and Malaysia by Berkeley Books, and in South Africa by Real Books.

Cover photography by Larry Kunkel
Styling by Veronica Randall

Library of Congress Cataloging-in-Publication Data
Pond, Lily
Pillow: exploring the heart of eros: a yellow silk book / by Lily Pond
    p.   cm.
Includes bibliographical references and index
ISBN 0-89087-858-7 (pbk.)
1. Sex—Quotations, maxims, etc.   I. Title.
        PN6084.S49P55   1998
    306.7—dc21   98-11915
                            CIP

First printing, 1998
Printed in Hong Kong

1 2 3 4 5 6 - 03 02 01 00 99 98

contents

to William & Robert
with thanks
for lessons
in love

introduction

In the course of our work and worry worlds sometimes we find
ourselves feeling like we've turned to stone. In order to reach
through to the heart of eros that lives within each of us, and
to stay in touch with it not only during your intimate times,
but throughout all of every day, and to keep in touch with that
for the rest of your life, the thing to do is to begin to start learning
how to dissolve the stone. Here is a book filled with sayings,
poems, and things to do together that will help you to begin to
do that by getting in touch again with yourself, with nature,
and with each other. Let it all be filled with joy.

EROS

that which draws us together

~

THIS IS A BOOK TO
READ OUT LOUD,
AND TO DO,
TO DRAW YOU TOGETHER.

love

of

nature

of

love

the breeze at dawn ripples the sheets...

Thom Ward

What I want is to see your face
in a tree, in the sun coming out,
in the air.

— RUMI

Our sheets smell more of sky and our bodies speak,
each crevice and plane and hump, as we snore and breathe,
and the stars that drag the season forward
flicker across the ceiling.

— RITA GABIS

Strip Stargazing

GO SOMEWHERE FAR FROM CITY LIGHTS DURING A METEOR SHOWER
(LISTED BELOW). DRAG YOUR SLEEPING BAGS OR MATTRESS
WHERE YOU CAN JUST LIE ON YOUR BACKS AND WATCH THE SKY
AND HAVE ALL THE PRIVACY YOU MIGHT EVER WANT.
EACH TIME EITHER OF YOU SEES A SHOOTING STAR YOU HAVE
TO TAKE OFF AN ITEM OF CLOTHING.

ANNUAL METEOR SHOWERS:

Quadrantids	Jan. 3-4
Lyrids	Apr. 21-22
Eta Aquarids	May 5-6
Delta/Iota Aquarids	July 29-30
Perseids	Aug. 11-12
Orionids	Oct. 21-22
Taurids	Nov. 4-5
Leonids	Nov. 16-17
Geminids	Dec. 13-14
Ursids	Dec. 22-23

"There are flowers for everyone in these hills,"
SAYS GINA COVINA. DISCUSS.

The Circle

SIT BACK TO BACK WITH YOUR LOVER. LOOK AS FAR TO YOUR
RIGHT AS YOU CAN. FOLLOW THE WHOLE 180° CIRCLE
OF YOUR VISION, SLOWLY. EACH TIME YOUR EYES FALL ON A
LIVING THING, A TREE, A BIRD, A FLOWER, CONSCIOUSLY FALL
IN LOVE. THEN TURN AROUND AND COMPLETE THE CIRCLE.

Surely all Being at bottom is happy.
– JANE HIRSHFIELD

WHEN YOU MAKE LOVE ALLOW IN
THE TREE BLOWING IN THE WIND.
ALLOW IN THE PLANTING OF A SEED,
ITS ROOTING AND ITS FLOWERING.
ALLOW YOURSELVES TO BECOME COVERED
IN GRASS GROWING OVER YOUR SKIN.
ALLOW THE CLOUDS TO PASS OVERHEAD.

~

The voice said, Cry. And he said, What shall I cry?
All flesh is grass, all the goodness
thereof is as the flower of the field.

– ISAIAH 40: 6-8

An affectionate ear on the belly must alter
The conception of the earth
pressing itself against the sky.
An elbow bent across the chest must anticipate
Early light angled over the lake. The curl of the pea
Can be understood as one hand
caught carefully inside another.

– PATTIANN ROGERS

MAKE LOVE AS BEINGS OF WATER.
MAKE LOVE AS BEINGS OF EARTH.
MAKE LOVE AS BEINGS OF FIRE.
MAKE LOVE AS BEINGS OF AIR.

Love might lead us again to the heart of the world.

– WILHELM BÖLSCHE

❧

Rise up, my love, my fair one, and come away.
For, lo, the winter is past, the rain is over and gone;
the flowers appear on the earth; the time of
the singing of birds is come and the
voice of the turtle is heard in our land.
The fig tree putteth forth her green figs, and
the vines with the tender grape give a good smell.
Arise, my love, my fair one, and come away.

– SONG OF SOLOMON 2: 10-12

In the mother's womb e'er waiting,
Lovely queen of field and lea,
Silent, great, all-animating
Nature carries thee and me.

– HÖLDERIN

LIE FACE TO FACE PRESSED AS TIGHTLY TOGETHER AS POSSIBLE,
AS TIGHTLY AS IF SPIDERS HAD ENCASED YOU IN WEB OR
MOTHS THEIR COCOON. PRESSED THIS WAY,
FEEL ALL THE WORLD YOU ARE NOT THAT SURROUNDS YOU,
THAT CRADLES YOU, THAT PUSHES YOU TOGETHER.

Let Nature Speak

GO SOMEWHERE WHERE THERE ARE FEWER BUILDINGS, ROADS WITH CARS, CONCRETE STRUCTURES. GO SOMEWHERE WHERE THINGS GROW — THE COUNTRY, THE MOUNTAINS, THE GRASSLANDS, THE OCEANSIDE, OR EVEN A CITY PARK. WITHOUT SPEAKING, POINT TO THINGS THAT EXPRESS YOUR FEELINGS FOR EACH OTHER. LET THE POINTING OF A FINGER SAY, "MY LOVE FOR YOU IS STRONG AND BEAUTIFUL AS THAT TREE," OR "MY FEELINGS FOR YOU ARE AS FRAGILE AND EXQUISITE AS THE EDGE OF THE POPPY'S PETAL."

Axis

I tongue
    I body
        I sun-bone
Through the conduits of night
        Spring of bodies
You night of wheat
        You forest in the sun
You waiting water
        You kneading-trough
of bones
Through the conduits of sun

        My night in your night
My sun in your sun
        My wheat in your
    kneading-trough
Your forest in my tongue
        Through the conduits
    of the body
Water in the night
        Your body in my body
Spring of bones
        Spring of suns.

– OCTAVIO PAZ

Sun

STAND BESIDE YOUR LOVER, FACING THE SETTING SUN.
CLOSE YOUR EYES AND HOLD HANDS. THROUGH THE THIN
MEMBRANES OF YOUR EYELIDS YOU WILL FEEL THE GOLD
OF THE SUN ENTER YOUR BODY. FEEL THE SUN ENTER
THROUGH YOUR FOREHEAD AND FILL YOU WITH ITS HEAT
AND GLORY. FEEL THE SUN COME INTO YOUR ARMS AND
HANDS. FEEL IT IN YOUR NECK AND CHEST. FEEL THE SUN
IN YOUR BELLY, BETWEEN YOUR LEGS, IN YOUR THIGHS,
FILL YOUR LEGS AND FEET. THEN FEEL THE HEAT YOUR
LOVER IS ALSO GATHERING PASS THROUGH THEIR HAND TO
YOURS AND BACK AGAIN. WHEN THE SUN HAS FINALLY SET
TURN TO EACH OTHER AND, WITH YOUR EYES STILL
CLOSED, TOUCH TOGETHER AT THE FOREHEAD. ABSORB
EVERYTHING THAT IS THERE.

every day you play
  with the light of the universe

Pablo Neruda

The Most Ancient Names of Fire

Blessed are the lovers
for theirs is the
    grain of sand
that sustains the center
    of the seas.

Dazed by the play
    of fountains
they hear nothing
but the music sprinkled by
their names.

Trembling

they cling to one another
like small frightened animals who
tremble, knowing they will die.

Nothing is alien to them.

Their only strength against
the wind and tide
are the beautifying words of
all existence: I love you.
We shall grow old together
to the end.

— ROBERTO SOSA

Let our dusts be one.

– *STEVE KOWIT*

AFTER GOVINDADASA

STAND FACING EACH OTHER NEAR A WINDOW, WHERE THE ONLY
ILLUMINATION ON YOUR FACES COMES FROM THE SKY.
REPEAT TO EACH OTHER, EACH STATEMENT SAID TWICE,
FIRST BY ONE, THEN BY THE OTHER:
"YOU WERE GIVEN TO ME BY THE SUN."
"YOU WERE GIVEN TO ME BY THE MOON."
"YOU WERE GIVEN TO ME BY THE STARS."
"YOU WERE GIVEN TO ME BY THE EARTH."

This autumn will end.
Nothing can last forever.
Fate controls our lives.
Fondle my living breasts
With your strong hands.

— *YOSANO AKIKO*

REFLECT ON SOMETHING YOU HAVE LOST.
HOLD EACH OTHER AT THAT MOMENT
AND RECOGNIZE SOMETHING YOU HAVE.

Seasonal Love

MAKE LOVE LIKE WINTER: COLDLY.
MAKE LOVE LIKE SPRING —
FINDING DELIGHT IN EACH NEW ACTION.
MAKE LOVE LIKE SUMMER: HOTLY.
MAKE LOVE LIKE AUTUMN — LINGERINGLY SLOW,
AS THOUGH IT MAY BE THE LAST TIME.

LIE OUTDOORS IN A QUIET PLACE ON A BLANKET ON THE GROUND.
EACH TIME YOU HEAR A BIRD, SING THE SONG TO THE OTHER.
TAKE TURNS IMITATING THE BIRDS.

Anything worth doing well is worth doing slowly.
– GYPSY ROSE LEE

ALL CREATION COMES FROM THE JOINING OF TWO PARTS.

sheets creamy in the moonlight...

John Goldfine

21

animals

such as we are

Put down your books —
you work all day!
It's sunny outside &
I want to play!
    – *PHOEBE BLACK*

~

happiness! it is December very cold,
we woke early this morning,
and lay in bed kissing,
our eyes squinched up like bats.
    – *ROBERT HASS*

...Suddenly you're lions
turning each other over in the dust...
he's a poppy
and so are you
and your passion
is reduced to tossing pollen
at each other's stamens
under a sky so clear
it reminds you of water
which it is, of course,
and now the two of you are fish...

– MARY MACKEY

Night Talk in a Dream Chamber

Whether by sea or river or in mountains,
a monk in the world abandons fame and fortune.
Every night we nestle like ducks in bed, sharing
intimate whispers, our bodies become at one.

– IKKYU SOJUN

BEHAVE LIKE SNAKES WITH EACH OTHER.
BEHAVE LIKE BEARS.

BE BORN ANEW;
LICK EACH OTHER
ALL CLEAN.

Give me the starlings that crouch in your shoulders
and the swallows that sleep in your feet.

– ROBERTA WERDINGER

BEHAVE LIKE BIRDS WITH EACH OTHER.
IMAGINE YOU ARE FLYING.

I believe when I came to you in your sleep,
when I was long awake, when I roused you half into
the world the robins weave their flights in,
that we too were literally aloft, that I licked awake
the wings from your shoulders, and we turned
and slanted and coasted down the same long breezes
as any birds, swallowed by the air, and believing.

– ROBERT WRIGLEY

❧

The mourning dove waits
in the warm grass
knowing its mate will come.

– PHOEBE BLACK

One Hundred Kisses

MAKE UP A HUNDRED NEW KINDS OF KISSES: KISS LIKE
A PENGUIN, WITH THE BACK OF THE HAND, KISS LIKE A
LATE-SUMMER BIRCH, HAIR GRACING EACH OTHER'S BODIES.
KISS LIKE A CAT, BUMPING AND MARKING. KISS LIKE WATER,
THE LIGHTEST TOUCHES MISSING NOWHERE. MAKE UP
NINETY-SIX MORE: OPEN YOUR EYES, SEE WHAT'S AROUND YOU,
KISS LIKE EVERYTHING IN THE WORLD.

kisses are a better fate
than wisdom
– E. E. CUMMINGS

Kisses. They bring me back to life.
– GEORGE SAND

❧

With a kiss let us set out for an unknown world.
– ALFRED DE MUSSET

❧

I look up from my work.
The House Finch is all decked out
in its orange feathers;
how can I work?
– PHOEBE BLACK

Pretend my body is the zoo and you're letting all the animals out.
Pretend you're handing me a diploma with your tongue.
Pretend you're climbing a mountain whose summit is inside me.
Pretend you're giving birth to me.
Pretend my body is an instrument you're tuning.
Pretend my body is a bowl of ice cream.
Pretend you're plucking fruit from my limbs.
Pretend we're swimming in each other's skin.
Pretend pulling away hurts.
Pretend you're a satellite probing for stars.
Pretend you don't know what you're doing.
Pretend you'll never be able to do this again.
Pretend we're the last tigers on earth.
Pretend we've exchanged bodies.

Pretend you don't know me.
Pretend you'll never see me again.
Pretend you're dreaming.
Pretend my body is God listening.
Pretend we're a confluence of rivers.
Pretend we're covered in feathers.
Pretend my body is a saxophone; a drum.
Pretend we're slugs.
Pretend you're inventing a recipe with my ingredients.
Pretend you've found what you want.
Pretend my body is what you like to wear most.
Pretend my body holds the cure.

– GWYNN O'GARA

Western wind, when wilt thou blow

that the small winds down can rain?

Oh, that my love were in my arms

and I in my bed again.

in all things

physical

we find

spirit

If some sins are truly jubilations,
then with you here beside me again
tonight, I'm certain I offend
many gods myself. I confess it and repent,
repent with the most contrite
voice I can manage, pulling my pillow
over my face, lying on my hands to try
to stop this rude sacrilege, my uncontrollable
crooning of happiness, incessant caressing.
touching your body everywhere, a sliding
vine of butterfly pea openly curling,
binding, such decadent opulence, my long,
excessive murmurs of immeasurable
adoration.

– PATTIANN ROGERS

Don't be satisfied with stories, how things
have gone with others. Unfold
your own myth, without complicated explanation,
so everyone will understand the passage,
WE HAVE OPENED YOU.

– RUMI

The beautiful presence came, as he touched her in the womb, and like spring
burst forth. I am creation. From her came the universe, that was the roar.
From her came worlds, she was their door. Spread across the galaxies, she
moved her body slowly, coming everywhere, at once, very wise. • In the beat
of moons, not seconds, he stroked her, so say the Scriptures.

– WILLIAM KOTZWINKLE

Art begins with the body and ends with the body.
– STANLEY BURNSHAW

~

PURE VULNERABILITY IS THE TRUEST APHRODISIAC.

~

LOSE YOURSELVES TOGETHER IN ANOTHER PLACE,
ANOTHER BEING, THAT IS YOUTWO,
SOMEWHERE ELSE, SOMETHING ELSE ENTIRELY.

Practice edgelessness.

PRACTICE JOY AND GRIEF. BECOME THEM WITH YOUR ENTIRE BODY.
BECOME THEM WITH YOUR ENTIRE BODIES TOGETHER.
THEY ARE THE SAME THING.

❖

*The soul can never be more than what
the body believes of itself.*

– PATTIANN ROGERS

*Love is the natural condition of our being revealed
when all else is relinquished.
Love is not what we become
but who we already are.*

– STEPHEN LEVINE

∼

THE ONLY PATH TO *Joy* IS *Surrender*.
THE ONLY PATH TO *Bliss* IS *Surrender*.
THERE IS BUT ONE CHOICE.

∼

The body makes love possible.

– GALWAY KINNELL

There is nothing to explain to you,
no trick to this desire.
I cannot own you.
I cannot save you.
There is no door left open but love

– PETER KUNZ

The flesh forgives everything.

– WANDA COLEMAN

Everything is known inside the skin.

– THAISA FRANK

Substance Massage

SPEND A DAY TRADING MASSAGES. ASSEMBLE THE FOLLOWING:
BABY POWDER, SAND, AND MUD. MAKE SURE YOU HAVE A SPOT
WHERE YOU CAN MAKE A BIG MESS, AND WHERE A SHOWER
IS CLOSE BY. ALTERNATING WITH EACH OTHER AS GIVER AND
TAKER OF MASSAGE, START WITH THE TALC. MASSAGE THE FEET,
THEN THE HANDS, THEN THE BOTTOM, THE CHEST, AND LAST,
THE STOMACH. DO EACH SPOT SLOWLY. FEEL CLEARLY HOW
EACH SPOT RESPONDS TO EACH SUBSTANCE — BOTH TO GIVE
AND TO TAKE. WHEN BOTH OF YOU HAVE EXPERIENCED ALL
THREE SUBSTANCES SHOWER YOURSELVES CLEAN AND
EXPERIENCE WATER AS ANOTHER SUBSTANCE.

In his book of the same name,
Thomas Centolella quotes Baal Shem Tov:
"Alas! the world is full of enormous lights and mysteries,
and man shuts them from himself with one small hand."
Remove the hand from your eyes.
See each other's lights and mysteries.

Whenever the unbelievable visits us,
we fall in love.

– DAVE HOWELL

from the quiz "Do You Know the Facts of Life?"

YOU HAVE ALMOST FINISHED THE EXAM. CONCLUDE IT
BY SITTING QUIETLY IN A LOTUS POSITION. CLOSE YOUR EYES
AND CONTEMPLATE THE TEN THOUSAND SENSUOUS THINGS
IN THE PHYSICAL WORLD. DON'T TALLY YOUR SCORE.

Notice the white throat of an iris,
the quiver of emerald hummingbirds,
the rolling gold hills of California summer
studded with live oaks.
(What do you consider the most voluptuous season?
Don't rest with the obvious.
Maybe it's the late yielding light of autumn,
the intimacy in that clarity, the sharpness of light
that brings everything closer.)

Consider the texture of thin silk velvet,
consider the scent of star jasmine,
Billie Holiday's voice,
any serious tenor saxophonist playing "Body and Soul,"
Edward Weston's nudes,
Georgia O'Keeffe's orchids and lilies.
Consider your childhood,
the shapes of light in the room,
the attentions and rhythms of speech,
the fluxes and cuttings, the touch.
This is the paradise where generosity begins.
Swim with me, swim with me,
These are the facts of life.
Now, come to your senses.

– LYNN LURIA-SUKENICK

Below me, fresh sheets.
Above me, you.

juice

and all things wet

ROLL NAKED IN THE MORNING DEW.

~

Find the Perfume

GO SOMEWHERE
WHERE YOU CAN BE OUTSIDE AND
IT IS WARM AND PRIVATE AND
YOU CAN TAKE OFF YOUR CLOTHES.
EACH OF YOU HAS HIDDEN A DROP OF
PERFUME ON YOUR BODY; THE OTHER MUST FIND IT.

~

Open me, river me, do what you will.

– ROBERTA WERDINGER

How I want what the first fruits bring. The first fruit
was the apple, wasn't it? Its juices anointing our bodies;
its skin red from our blushes and rubs. Skin like our
polished bones; its white inner body, with open pores,
what teeth sink into; its core, the heart
and stalk of this life, wild in seed.

– ED KLEINSCHMIDT

A person is like a fruit which will only yield
its fragrance when rubbed by the hands.

– adapted from THE PERFUMED GARDEN

I thought I would love you forever —
and just a little, I may,
in the way I still move towards a crate, knees bent,
or reach for a man: as one might stretch
for the three or four fruits that lie
in the sun at the top
of the tree, too ripe for any moment but this,
that open their skin at first touch, yielding sweetness,
sweetness and heat, and in me, each time since,
the answering yes.

– JANE HIRSHFIELD

Let's bless the body before love.
By rights we should, every detail.
We could use water, spring water
or rose, minted or bay rum. A touch
to the shoulders — BLESS THESE.
A drop behind each knee — SANCTIFY HERE.
A sprinkle to the belly, yours, mine —
IN HEARTFELT APPRECIATION.

– PATTIANN ROGERS

≈

We are water. We are swept away.
Desire begins in wetness.

– TERRY TEMPEST WILLIAMS

49

Speaking in Tongues

We were speaking in tongues.
We were rolling in the sheets, our tongues were driven
mad with Pentecostal ecstasy, our tongues were epileptic,
our tongues were frothing, our tongues were crying,
our tongues were screaming, our tongues were babbling
holy nonsense, our tongues were repentant of every sin,
our tongues praised God, our tongues were baptized,
our tongues were washed with the Blood of the Lamb,
and our tongues were born again. And again.

– CARSON REED

LIE TOGETHER IN THE QUIET OF A DARK AFTERNOON. BREATHE
TOGETHER FOR THREE MINUTES, LISTENING. THEN BEGIN,
ALTERNATELY, TO USE YOUR TONGUE ON DIFFERENT SPOTS ON
YOUR LOVER. STOP BETWEEN EACH VISIT, TO SAVOR HOW IT
FELT, TO GIVE, TO RECEIVE, HOW EACH SPOT WAS DIFFERENT.

I hold your head tight
Between my thighs and press
Against your mouth and
Float away forever in
An orchid boat, on the River of Heaven.
– MARICHIKO

ONCE, AT LEAST ONCE IN YOUR LIFE, MAKE LOVE OUTDOORS NAKED IN A WARM RAIN. IF YOU JUST ABSOLUTELY NEVER HAVE WARM RAINS WHERE YOU LIVE, AND IF YOU CAN'T VISIT ANYWHERE THAT DOES, BUY A SPRINKLER.

I begin to believe the only sin
is distance, refusal.
All others stemming from this. Then, come.
Rivers, come. Irrevocable futures, come.
Come even joy.

– *JANE HIRSHFIELD*

Your shapes, my own,
we lie down, closing our eyes into the shapeless
ocean of movement under the sheet, not sleep,
not rest or conversation, only the wash
and wish of arms lightly over shoulders, hands
following a smoothness down, the belly, thighs
tightening, opening, tightening, opening.

JAMES CLARK ANDERSON

I want to do with you what spring does with cherry trees.

– PABLO NERUDA

Love Song

I love you, I love you, is my song
and here my silliness begins.

I love you, I love you my lung,
I love you, I love you my wild grapevine,
and if love is like wine:
you are my predilection
from your hands to your feet:
you are the wineglass of hereafter
and my bottle of destiny.

— PABLO NERUDA

Water Babies

BE TOGETHER IN THE WATER, IN THE OCEAN, A SEA,
A LAKE, A POOL. MOVE TOGETHER AS CLOSE TO EACH
OTHER AS YOU CAN WITHOUT TOUCHING. BE AWARE
THAT EVERY INCH OF YOU THAT IS TOUCHED BY WATER
IS AN EXTENSION OF THE TOUCH OF THE OTHER,
TOUCHING YOU EVERYWHERE A BEING CAN BE TOUCHED
ALL AT THE SAME TIME. YOUR LOVER HAS ENDLESS
HANDS, AND IS LEAVING YOU WANTING NOTHING.

What You Bring

STAND HAND IN HAND SOMEWHERE FACING A GREAT WIND,
ALONGSIDE A BAY, PERHAPS, OR AT THE OCEAN. CLOSE
YOUR EYES, AND SPREAD YOUR ARMS AS FAR AS POSSIBLE TO
CATCH AS MUCH WIND AS YOU CAN. BECOME AS A KITE:
PERHAPS IT WILL LIFT YOU. PERHAPS YOU WILL BECOME AS
WATER AND THE WIND WILL GO RIGHT THROUGH YOU.
ALLOW IT TO. WILL IT TO. BUT WAIT! IT WON'T.
FEEL THAT ONE SMALL WARM PLACE INSIDE THE WIND
WILL NOT PASS THROUGH, AND THAT IS EXACTLY WHAT YOU
BRING TO EACH OTHER WHEN YOU MAKE LOVE.

*your white shell spiraled
in moonlight
on the bed's white beach*

John Ciardi

song
&
dance

all the sounds and movement

ASSEMBLE A STACK OF CDs TOGETHER, YOURS AND SOME FROM
THE LIBRARY THAT YOU NORMALLY WOULD NEVER LISTEN TO.
AS MANY DIFFERENT KINDS OF MUSIC AS YOU CAN. THEN SPEND
AT LEAST ONE CUT OFF EACH DANCING TO THAT MUSIC.
LET YOUR BODIES GO WITH THE MUSIC.
FIND NEW BEINGS IN EACH OF YOU.

WILHELM BÖLSCHE SAYS, "FOLLOW THE BEE IN SPIRIT,
AND ITS SOFT, DREAMLIKE, DELICATE HUMMING WILL GROW
INTO A GIGANTIC MELODY FOR YOU." MAKE A DANCE TO
THAT MELODY, THEN LISTEN FOR YOUR OWN.

She does the red dress dance, sudden topaz turn,
pallid bellies of a thousand frogs dance.

– REGINA O'MELVENY

❧

We moved
ever so slightly. The house on its moorings creaked.
A little music from her throat, or was it coming
from the bay? We were two creatures floating.
Wetness everywhere, the whole world liquescent, delicious.
In a white room without time, we were tensed together
without need of time, my hands, my long hands on her face,
the heat there so familiar. Is this prayer, I wanted to know.
And she said, Yes, it is. Make it last forever.

– THOMAS CENTOLELLA

"DANCE WITH ABANDON," GEORGE BALANCHINE
TOLD SUZANNE FARRELL. ABANDON WHAT?
FIGURE THAT OUT AND ABANDON IT.

☙

I am dizzy. I am drunk with pleasure. There is no
need to speak.
Listen.
Below us.
Above us.
Inside us.
Come.
This is all there is.

– TERRY TEMPEST WILLIAMS

Dance

I was convinced I couldn't dance. Then I met a man who patiently taught me to dance a little. He made it fun, had a great sense of humor about it. The first time we danced in public I was so happy. We knew two steps, and we were just doing the same things over and over, but I was so giddy I was dizzy with it. I could only dance with a person I knew well. How can you follow a stranger, how can you possibly predict what he's about to do? I need to be able to read every little gesture and expression. It's such an intimate thing, following somebody's lead. We stare coldly into each other's eyes and waltz in these mad centrifugal circles exactly like we were one person. My face goes into his chest at exactly the right place. I have to go into a kind of trance to be able to follow him. If you think about it you'll stumble and mess up and step all over his feet. I used to try to count in my head. But now I've figured out this trance deal where my face is in his chest and it's the twilight zone, time has stopped, the moment lasts forever. I could die right there, my ears ringing with joy.

– ELIZABETH CHURCHILL

MAKE LOVE WITH YOUR EYES OPEN THE ENTIRE TIME.
MAKE LOVE WITH YOUR EYES CLOSED THE WHOLE TIME.
MAKE LOVE WITHOUT MAKING A SINGLE SOUND.
MAKE LOVE MAKING AS MANY SOUNDS AS POSSIBLE.

≈

Take off your clothes and behave like cats with
each other. After a while, behave like dogs.
Include all their noises.

≈

READ ALL THE POEMS AND STORIES IN THIS BOOK
OUT LOUD TO EACH OTHER.

The A-h-h-h-h-h Breath

STEPHEN LEVINE DEVELOPS THIS MORE FULLY, BUT I'LL GIVE
YOU A SIMPLIFIED VERSION: ONE OF YOU LIES COMFORTABLY ON
YOUR BACK WITH THE OTHER SITTING ALONGSIDE, NEAR THE
WAIST. BREATHE TOGETHER FOR A WHILE AND BE SURE BOTH OF
YOU ARE QUITE COMFORTABLE. AFTER A FEW MOMENTS, THE
ONE SITTING BEGINS TO TUNE INTO THE BREATHING OF THE ONE
LYING DOWN, FOLLOWING IT WITH HIS OWN BREATH — MORE
THAN SIMPLY GETTING "IN SYNC," IT'S STAYING IN TOUCH,
FOLLOWING ANY SMALL CHANGE IN THE PATTERN. AFTER A FEW
BREATHS, THE SITTING ONE ALLOWS A DEEP "AH-H-H-H-H" TO
COME FROM HIM AS HE EXHALES. THE LYING ONE IS SILENT, AND
JUST KEEPS BREATHING NORMALLY. THERE WILL COME A SENSE
OF BREATHING ONE BREATH. THE ONE LYING CAN STOP
WHENEVER SHE WISHES, AND LATER THEY CAN TRADE PLACES.

This morning I wished (once) to be a quiet
lover, but who can love with a closed mouth?
It opens, bites, is wet. The sounds come out.

– ELIZABETH ALEXANDER

❧

TAKE OFF YOUR CLOTHES.
LIE ONE FLAT OUT ON TOP OF THE OTHER.
HUM.

❧

And there is so much singing, so much night,
and nobody able to sleep.

– JOHN MINCZESKI

If you want to excite me not just for this moment
but so that I'll carry you inside of me,
and at a word entering grow hot for you,
then pull your hand back away from my body.
Talk to me.

– KATHRYN STEADMAN

You talked to me
as we made love, unhurried. The world is large,
and it is lovely to be kind to one another.

– CAROLYN MILLER

Do they train the rain in Spain to fall, to dance, on the hot plain?
Did you dance with the Basque men out into the sunlight? Did you
find green, full-blown roses behind the horses' ears? Did you shed
tears over every great expanse you felt as the little mute boys, barren
orange trees, little deaf girls? You danced long slow steps. Your feet
became blue as the Mediterranean. Dust in every crevice and you
searching for a wet tongue, a finger of red wine, skin you could read
dark news to, hair on fire that burns all night. Spain — you told me
of it and I watched your lips move, I watched your teeth flash and
your tongue flame, your breath boil me in your mouth. I watched
your body tell what your body knows — about Spain, Spain
— you spread yourself, imitating foreign countries.

– ED KLEINSCHMIDT

MAKE LOVE LIKE FRANCE.

MAKE LOVE LIKE JAPAN,

CHINA.

MAKE LOVE LIKE AFRICA,

LIKE BRAZIL,

MAKE LOVE

LIKE THE ANTARCTIC.

~

This pillow, this bed,
our ship on night's dark waters.

alone

together

Love Letters

WRITE LOVE LETTERS TO EACH OTHER. THINK OF ALL THE VERY
SPECIFIC THINGS YOU CAN. THE WAY THE OTHER WALKS.
THE WAY THEY MAKE JELLY SANDWICHES. SHOW HOW CLOSELY
YOU HAVE NOTICED. LIST EVERYTHING. LEAVE NOTHING OUT.
I LOVE HOW YOUR SKIN LOOKS IN THAT GREEN SHIRT. I LOVE
HOW EXPRESSIVE YOUR HAND IS WHEN WE WALK HOLDING
HANDS. I LIKED WATCHING YOU PLAY IN THE WAVES. I LIKE HOW
YOU TALK TO STRANGERS. THE SHAPE OF YOUR SHOULDERS.
YOUR FEET. TAKE A LOT OF TIME. WHEN YOU'RE BOTH ALL
DONE EXCHANGE THEM AND EACH READ THEIR OWN LETTER
OUT LOUD TO THE WRITER, BUT CHANGE EVERY "YOU" TO "I"
AND EVERY "I" TO A "YOU." "YOU LOVE THE WAY I MAKE JELLY
SANDWICHES." ALLOW YOURSELF TO REALLY FEEL EACH
STATEMENT. LET EACH STATEMENT BE A GIFT.

MAKE LOVE WITH YOUR PARTNER EXACTLY AS USUAL.
PAY VERY CLOSE ATTENTION TO EVERYTHING YOUR PARTNER
DOES TO YOU AND HOW THEY DO IT.
THEN MAKE LOVE WITH YOUR PARTNER AGAIN, ONLY THIS TIME
BE EACH OTHER. DO EVERYTHING TO YOUR PARTNER
EXACTLY THE WAY THEY DO IT TO YOU.

❧

PRESS TOGETHER THE PARTS OF YOUR BODIES THAT CONTAIN YOUR
HEARTS. FEEL THEM BEAT TOGETHER. BECOME SIAMESE
TWINS AS YOUR TWO HEARTS GROW INTO ONE.

We dressed each other
Hurrying to say farewell
In the depth of night.
Our drowsy thighs touched and we
Were caught in bed by the dawn.

– *EMPRESS EIFUKU*

❖

Write three tiny secrets your lover doesn't know.
Trade papers.

PLAY MIRROR. SIT CROSS-LEGGED IN FRONT OF EACH OTHER. ALTERNATE THE ROLE OF "INSTIGATOR." FEEL EACH OTHER'S MOVEMENTS COMING OUT THROUGH YOUR OWN BODY. REVERSE.

∾

SIT CROSS-LEGGED ACROSS FROM EACH OTHER AND LOOK INTO EACH OTHER'S EYES. PRACTICE THIS MANY TIMES, IN MANY PLACES, UNTIL YOU CAN LOOK AT EACH OTHER FOR A LONG TIME.

∾

We need a softer, slower word
                    for seeing.
– *ANTHONY ROBBINS*

Not speaking of the way,
Not thinking of what comes after,
Not questioning name or fame,
Here, loving love,
You and I look at each other.

— *YOSANO AKIKO*

Breathe.

SIT FACING EACH OTHER ON THE BED. LOOK EACH OTHER IN THE EYES, AND JUST LOOK FOR A WHILE. IT'S JUST YOU — JUST YOU TWO IN THE WHOLE WORLD. FOR THE MOMENT, ANYONE IN YOUR HOUSE ISN'T THERE. YOUR NEIGHBORS ON ALL SIDES, JUST FOR THE MOMENT, ARE NOT THERE. YOUR WHOLE TOWN IS NOT THERE. YOUR STATE; YOUR COUNTRY; YOUR HEMISPHERE; YOUR WORLD. YOU TWO ARE THE ONLY TWO PEOPLE IN THE WHOLE WORLD. HOLD THAT FEELING FOR A NUMBER OF MINUTES.

THEN ALLOW BACK THE PEOPLE WHO MAKE MUSIC. ALLOW IN THE PEOPLE WHO MAKE CHILDREN AND THOSE WHO TEACH THEM. ALLOW BACK THE OTHER LOVERS; ALLOW BACK THE GARDENERS AND THE CHEFS AND THE BOOKSELLERS. BRING BACK THE ARTISTS, THE DANCERS, THOSE WHO BRING LIGHT, AND MAIL, AND WATER, AND BRING BACK

THE GRANDPARENTS AND THE AUNTS AND UNCLES
AND COUSINS ON TO THE FIFTH AND SIXTH REMOVE.

THERE YOU ARE. JUST YOU TWO,
AND A WORLD OF OTHERS WHO HELP YOU TO LOVE.

~

If ever we move from here, this room,
this light, this time of waking up with you,
not conscious or intelligible, is what
I want to bring with us to the next world.

– JAMES CLARK ANDERSON

Love me. At this moment we
Are the happiest
People in the world.

❧

Lovers don't finally meet somewhere.
They are in each other all along.

— RUMI

❧

There is an eros present at every meeting.

— SUSAN GRIFFIN

ARRANGE TO MEET FOR DINNER SOMEWHERE YOU HAVE
NEVER BEEN IN AN UNFAMILIAR PART OF TOWN. ARRIVE
THERE SEPARATELY. BE ON TIME. THIS IS NOT AN EXERCISE
IN "ATTEMPTING TO PICK UP A 'STRANGER.'" THIS IS AN
EXERCISE IN RECOGNIZING YOUR BELOVED. NOTICE HOW
YOU FEEL ALONE IN A NEW PLACE. NOTICE YOUR
ANTICIPATION. NOTICE WHAT YOU SEE WHEN YOU FIRST
SEE THE PERSON YOU ARE WAITING FOR. NOTICE HOW
THEY APPEAR DIFFERENT IN A NEW PLACE. NOTICE HOW
YOU FEEL WHEN THEY ARE FINALLY SEATED BEFORE YOU.

~

See each other.

A Beloved Meditation

*Stephen Levine develops this more fully;
this is a very simplified version:*

SIT CROSS-LEGGED FACING EACH OTHER, EYES CLOSED.
ENVISION YOUR LOVER'S FACE IN YOUR MIND, DETAIL BY
DETAIL, FEATURE BY FEATURE, AS CLEARLY AS POSSIBLE.
THEN OPEN YOUR EYES. SEE HOW THE REALITY COMPARES
WITH THE IMAGE. LET ALL OF THE IMAGES GO. SIMPLY SEE,
AND LET YOURSELF BE SEEN. LET GO OF ANYTHING THAT
ARISES TO INTERFERE WITH YOUR SIMPLY SEEING. LET YOUR
MIND GO. SEE ONLY WITH YOUR HEART. THIS IS YOUR
BELOVED. THIS IS YOUR BELOVED. LET GO.

Renaming of the Parts

WITHOUT YOUR CLOTHES, BEARING MAGNIFYING GLASSES
AND VERY SENSITIVE FINGERS, EXAMINE EACH OTHER'S
BODIES VERY CAREFULLY. MISS NOTHING. RENAME ANY PART
YOU FEEL, UPON THOROUGH EXAMINATION, HAS BEEN
MIS-NAMED. DRAW PICTURES OF EACH OTHER — ACCURACY
IS NOT IMPORTANT — AND LABEL THE PARTS WITH THE NEW
NAMES SO YOU WON'T FORGET.

Tell each other everything you know
about each other. You put salt on your salmon.
You use the brush on your back in the shower.
You wear only black socks. Everything.

The True Weight of the Body

LIE ON YOUR BACKS BESIDE EACH OTHER. ALLOW YOUR MUSCLES TO RELAX FULLY AND HOLD NO TENSION, TO BE HEAVY, TO BE CLAY. THEN, ONE BY ONE, TAKE THE MEASURE OF YOUR LOVE. LIFT THE ARM AND TEST IT IN YOUR HANDS; FEEL ITS HEFT AND WARMTH, THEN LAY IT DOWN GENTLY. TEST THE HAND, THE HEAD, THE LEG AND FOOT. GET TO KNOW THE SHEER BODY-NESS OF YOUR LOVE, THE STUFF OF WHICH THE BODY'S MADE. AND THEN REVERSE.

How brilliantly we communicated
right to the candle's sticky end,
in this new language
of weight and counterweight,
of lift and tilt and press.

— MEG HILL FITZ-RANDOLPH

SAY: I TOUCH YOUR ARM WITH MY HAND.
SAY: I FEEL THE TOUCH OF YOUR HAND ON MY ARM.
SAY: YOUR ARM FEELS ......
SAY: YOUR HAND FEELS ......
TRY MANY COMBINATIONS.

Sit facing each other, cross-legged, eyes closed.
Breathe together for a few moments.
Begin to speak to each other. Both
continue to speak, saying everything, letting
everything pour out. Do not stop to listen or
to respond. Continue until there is nothing more to say.

Together we catch our breath,
hear the pulse, our hearts, stumble down
into the stillness after passion.

– *THERESA VINCIGUERRA*

Alien Planet

LIE ON YOUR BACK IN THE DARK WITH YOUR EYES CLOSED
IN A ROOM JUST SLIGHTLY TOO COOL FOR COMFORT WITH ONE
LESS COVERLET THAN YOU NEED. FEEL YOUR ALONENESS
AS IT TRAVELS THROUGH YOUR BLOODSTREAM. YOU ARE ON
THE MOON AND YOU ARE TOTALLY ALONE. SUDDENLY YOU
THINK YOU HEAR SOMETHING MOVING, SOMETHING BREATHING.
YOU REACH OUT YOUR HAND AND FEEL SOMETHING WARM,
AND SOFT. EYES STILL CLOSED, EXPLORE THAT ALIEN LIFE
FORM. HOW SWEET IT IS. BONES UNDER THE SKIN.
HOW COMPLEX AND HOW GENTLE.

While I work in the dark
front of the house,
the back of the house,
where you are,
is flooded with light.
I grab you,
abandoning everything,
taken by sunlight.

– *PHOEBE BLACK*

light opens the folds of the sheets

Octavio Paz

isn't it all

delicious

?

sweetness dripping down
you fluttering on my mouth
— CAROLE MASO

~

Sweet Suckle

GO TO THE GROCERY STORE OR PRODUCE MARKET OR
FARMERS MARKET TOGETHER AND PICK AS MANY FOODS
AS YOU CAN FIND THAT CAN BE EATEN WITHOUT THE TEETH.
FIND PEACHES AND BANANAS, FIND YOGURT AND PUDDING
AND CREAM. BRING EVERYTHING HOME AND HAVE A
WONDROUS LUNCH, NEVER USING YOUR TEETH.

Black Tea

It's a good night

because you were free with me,
because you let me cry on your gold chains
that led to my village. The two of us up there
for a look, you know the place where the sheep are born
and the goat milk is fresh, with you it felt like fruit

going back and forth across me on a silk boat, your eyelashes
suddenly bare and a message, the song
that tensed my neck with its I'm-not-a-child-anymore teeth, steamed
into worlds of honey.

— JANE MILLER

Honey

CALL EACH OTHER HONEY. TOUCH EACH OTHER WITH HONEY.
PUT HONEY ON THE PALMS OF YOUR HANDS AND STROKE
EACH OTHER. THEN CLEAN EACH OTHER OF HONEY.

❧

food colorings etching into each other,
eggs being folded into batter,
we are greens wilting at the steam
giving up our identities
in the name of the greater lunch.

– PHOEBE BLACK

I wanted to be the forms of light, to be the wind,
the vision, to burn you like a star, to wrap you in storm,
to make the tree yield. I wanted to drown in your
white water, and where your fingers probed I wanted
to hear each pore cry out, "Open, Open. Break Open!
Let nothing be hidden or closed."

– DEENA METZGER

❧

HAVE A LUNCH OR DINNER OF ALL OF THE FOODS YOU FIND
MOST AKIN TO LOVEMAKING, MAYBE OYSTERS AND PERSIMMONS,
MAYBE FRESH CARROTS AND CAKE. THEN MAKE LOVE: SAY,
"THIS IS THE PERSIMMON," OR "THIS IS THE FROSTING,"
AND BE IT WITH EACH OTHER.

Recommended Futurist Recipes for Love

1. Eat large oysters, drops of Muscat wine from Syracuse mixed into their seawater.

2. Remove the yolks from eggs, fill them with plum jam, hide them amidst bananas in plain ice cream.

3. Fill little tubes of pastry with many different flavors, one of plums, one of apples cooked in rum, one of potatoes drenched in cognac, one of sweet rice.

4. Mix eggs, lemon juice, flour and oil to a thin batter. Pluck the heads of full-blooming red roses. Deep-fry them and serve with rice pudding made with coffee, lemon, and the water of orange flowers.

— MARINETTI

NAME THE THINGS YOU DO WITH YOUR MOUTH. DO THEM.

❖

Where You Stop for Lunch

IT MATTERS. YOU WILL ALWAYS REMEMBER.
WRITE DOWN EVERYWHERE YOU'VE EVER EATEN TOGETHER.
MAKE THE LIST TOGETHER.

❖

EAT LIKE HORSES.

Menu Poem

Without your clothes, taste each other. All over.
After an Indian restaurant and curries,
take off your clothes and taste each other. All over.
Then go to a Mexican restaurant and eat chiles.
Two hours later:
Take off your clothes and taste each other. All over.
(You do not have to do all of these on the same day)

~

Peel each other.

I love couscous, watermelon, getting up early in the morning, preachers,
rivers, music, presents, persimmons, paris, purple, pottery, sun ra,
sardines and grits, cherokees, robert, paul laurence dunbar, puerto ricans,
sassafras tea, kane, the mediterranean, lace curtains, bustelo coffee,
children, getting letters, turnip greens, silver and....

– VERTA MAE GROSVENOR

❧

The faith we put in a lover's mouth!

– STEPHEN DUNN

you ask me about blessings
i tell you about what our bed whispered to me
in the middle of the night

permissions

For more information on works listed below, see pages 104–106.

Page 4.   Thom Ward, from the poem "The Breeze at Dawn" [*Seven Hundred Kisses: A Yellow Silk Book*]. Reprinted by permission of the author.

Page 5.   Rumi, translation by Coleman Barks and John Moyne [*The Erotic Spirit: An Anthology of Poems of Sensuality, Love and Longing*]. Reprinted by permission of the translator.

Page 5.   Rita Gabis, from the poem "Sleeping Together" [*Yellow Silk: Journal of Erotic Arts*]. Reprinted by permission of the author.

Page 7.   Gina Covina, from a story title [*Yellow Silk: Journal of Erotic Arts*]. Reprinted by permission of the author.

Page 7.   Jane Hirshfield, from the poem "Percolation" [*Yellow Silk: Journal of Erotic Arts*]. Reprinted by permission of the author.

Page 9.   Pattiann Rogers, from the poem "The Question of Affection" [*Firekeeper*]. Reprinted by permission of the author.

Page 10.   Wilhelm Bölsche [*Love-Life in Nature*].

Page 11.   Hölderin [*Love-Life in Nature*].

Page 13.   Octavio Paz, trans. Eliot Weinberger, from the poem "Axis" [*A Draft of Shadows*]. Reprinted by permission of the publisher.

Page 15.   Pablo Neruda, trans. W.S. Merwin, from the poem "Every Day You Play" [*Twenty Love Poems*]. Reprinted by permission of the publisher.

Page 16. Roberto Sosa, trans. Jo Anne Engelbert, from the poem "The Most Ancient Names of Fire" [*The Erotic Spirit: An Anthology of Poems of Sensuality, Love and Longing*]. Reprinted by permission of Curbstone Press.

Page 17. Steve Kowit, after Govindadasa [*Yellow Silk: Journal of Erotic Arts*]. Reprinted by permission of the author.

Page 18. Yosano Akiko [*One Hundred More Poems from the Japanese*]. Reprinted by permission of the publisher.

Page 21. John Goldfine, from the story "A Sun to Shine on Them" [*Seven Hundred Kisses: A Yellow Silk Book*]. Reprinted by permission of the author.

Page 23. Robert Hass, from the poem "Happiness" [*Sun Under Wood*]. Reprinted by permission of the publisher.

Page 24. Mary Mackey, from the poem "Don't Start Something You Can't Finish" [*Yellow Silk: Journal of Erotic Arts*]. Reprinted by permission of the author.

Page 25. Ikkyu Sojun, trans. Sam Hamill [*The Erotic Spirit: An Anthology of Poems of Sensuality, Love and Longing*]. Reprinted by permission of the translator.

Page 26. Roberta Werdinger, from the poem "Poem" [*Yellow Silk: Journal of Erotic Arts*]. Reprinted by permission of the author.

Page 27. Robert Wrigley, from the poem "Flight" [*Yellow Silk: Journal of Erotic Arts*]. Reprinted by permission of the author.

Page 28. E.E. Cummings, from the poem "since feeling is first." Reprinted by permission of the publisher.

Page 30. Gwynn O'Gara, from the poem "The Manual of Ong" [*Yellow Silk: Journal of Erotic Arts*]. Reprinted by permission of the author.

Page 32. Traditional lyric.

Page 34. Pattiann Rogers, from the poem "Are Some Sins Hosannas" [*Firekeeper*]. Reprinted by permission of the author.

Page 35. Rumi, trans. John Moyne and Coleman Barks. Reprinted by permission of the translators.

Page 35. William Kotzwinkle, from the story "Jewel of the Moon" [*Yellow Silk: Journal of Erotic Arts*]. Reprinted by permission of Henry Dunow Literary Agency. The story also appears in *Yellow Silk Erotic Arts & Letters*.

Page 36. Stanley Burnshaw [*The Seamless Web*]. Reprinted by permission of the publisher.

Page 37. Pattiann Rogers, from the poem "The Grooming" [*Firekeeper*]. Reprinted by permission of the author.

Page 38. Stephen Levine [*Healing into Life and Death*]. Reprinted by permission of the publisher.

Page 38. Galway Kinnell, from an interview entitled "Walking Down the Stairs." Reprinted by permission of the author.

Page 39. Peter Kunz, from the poem "If I Could" [*Seven Hundred Kisses: A Yellow Silk Book*]. Reprinted by permission of the author.

Page 39. Wanda Coleman, from the poem "Mother the Flesh" [*Yellow Silk: Journal of Erotic Arts*]. Reprinted by permission of the author.

Page 39. Thaisa Frank, from the story "Animal Skins" [*Seven Hundred Kisses: A Yellow Silk Book*]. Reprinted by permission of the author.

Page 41. Dave Howell, from the poem of the same name [*Seven Hundred Kisses: A Yellow Silk Book*]. Reprinted by permission of the author.

Page 54. Pablo Neruda, translated by William O'Daly [*The Erotic Spirit: An Anthology of Poems of Sensuality, Love and Longing*]. Reprinted by permission of Copper Canyon Press.

Page 57. John Ciardi, from the poem "To Judith Asleep" [*Selected Poems*]. Reprinted by permission of the author's estate.

Page 59. Wilhelm Bölsche [*Love-Life in Nature*].

Page 60. Regina O'Melveny, from the poem "She Does the Red Dress Dance" [*Yellow Silk: Journal of Erotic Arts*]. Reprinted by permission of the author.

Page 60. Thomas Centolella, from the poem "As It Was in the Beginning" [*Lights & Mysteries*]. Reprinted by permission of the author.

Page 61. Terry Tempest Williams [*Desert Quartet*]. Reprinted by permission of the publisher.

Page 62. Elizabeth Churchill [The Well computer forum]. Reprinted by permission of the author.

Page 64. Stephen Levine [*Embracing the Beloved*]. Paraphrased by permission of the publisher.

Page 65. Elizabeth Alexander, from the poem "Sonnet" [*Yellow Silk: Journal of Erotic Arts*]. Reprinted by permission of the author.

Page 65. John Minczeski, from the poem "Orchid Flight" [*Yellow Silk: Journal of Erotic Arts*]. Reprinted by permission of the author.

Page 66. Kathryn Steadman, from the story "What She Wrote Him" [*Seven Hundred Kisses: A Yellow Silk Book*]. Reprinted by permission of the author.

Page 66. Carolyn Miller, from the poem "At the End of Summer" [*Yellow Silk: Journal of Erotic Arts*]. Reprinted by permission of the author.

The books in this list are here for several reasons. Some are quoted from directly in the text, some are not quoted directly, but directly inspired items in the text, and some I've included simply because I recommend them.

Aureole. Copyright © Carole Maso 1996; The Ecco Press.

The Book of Eros. Copyright © Lily Pond, ed. 1996; Crown Books.

Complete Poems: 1904–1962 by E.E. Cummings. Copyright © George James Firmage (editor). New York: Liveright Publishing Company, 1985. Poem copyright 1926, 1954, 1991 by the Trustees for the E.E. Cummings Trust.

Desert Quartet. Copyright © Terry Tempest Williams 1995; Pantheon.

A Draft of Shadows by Octavio Paz. Copyright © 1979; New Directions Publishing Corp. Poem copyright © The New Yorker Magazine, Inc. 1979.

Embracing the Beloved. Copyright © Stephen and Ondrea Levine 1995; Doubleday, a division of Bantam Doubleday Dell Publishing Group, Inc.

The Eros of Everyday Life. Copyright © Susan Griffin 1995; Doubleday, a division of Bantam Doubleday Dell Publishing Group, Inc.

The Erotic Impulse. Copyright © David Steinberg, ed. 1992; Tarcher.

The Erotic Spirit: An Anthology of Poems of Sensuality, Love and Longing. Copyright © Sam Hamill, ed. 1996; Shambhala.

Firekeeper. Copyright © Pattiann Rogers 1994; Milkweed Editions.

The Futurist Cookbook by Marinetti, trans. Suzanne Brill. Bedford Arts.

Healing into Life and Death. Copyright © Stephen Levine 1987; Anchor/Doubleday, a division of Bantam Doubleday Dell Publishing Group, Inc.

Hot Monogamy. Copyright © Patricia Love and Jo Robinson 1994; Dutton.

Keeping the Love You Find. Copyright © Harville Hendrix 1992; Pocket Books.

Landscape at the End of the Century. Copyright © Stephen Dunn 1991; W.W. Norton.

Lights & Mysteries. Copyright © Thomas Centolella 1995; Copper Canyon Press.

A Little Book of Sensual Comfort. Copyright © Jennifer Louden 1994; HarperSanFrancisco.

Love-Life in Nature by Wilhelm Bölsche. Albert & Charles Boni, 1926.